About the Author

Alexander Gunningham was inspired to write Harry's Stories - the Road to Recovery after being diagnosed with Chronic Myeloid Leukaemia in 2002. He felt the need to create something that has lasting social value whilst still being entertaining. He was encouraged and inspired by witnessing the stoicism, cheeriness and braveness by his fellow Leukaemiacs and other Cancer sufferers on the children's and adults' wards at his local hospital.

Alexander has been a professional writer since 1979, working as an award-winning advertising copywriter, as a journalist and scriptwriter for radio, TV and film. He is currently finishing writing a children's novel, entitled A Gnome Called Sponge, to be published by Auric Fusion Books in 2015.

Harry's Stories -
the Road To Recovery

Alexander Gunningham

Auric Fusion Books

Harry's Stories – the Road to Recovery.

Stories to Help Make Children Feel Better

by Alexander Gunningham.

Published by Auric Fusion Books as an electronic book in 2013.

Illustrations by Sue Pearson.

ISBN: 978-0-9931476-0-9

Printed in Great Britain by Biddles, King's Lynn, Norfolk PE32 1SF

Contents

Dedication

This book is respectfully dedicated to Sharry Clark – with grateful thanks for all of your support, help and loving kindnesses to many people and projects in many fields (and hedgerows).

Love and Light to you and to everybody, everywhere.

Foreword

These stories feature two principal characters: a young boy Johnny (who has an unspecified disease) and his teddy bear called Harry. At night, in Johnny's dreams, the pair have several adventures together.

Their exploits take part in a magical land within the dreamscape, called Happy Valley. There Harry introduces Johnny to new friends, most of whom are other bears.

Each new friend has a message of hope and wisdom for Johnny, expressed in simple terms that the youngest child of average intelligence will easily be able to grasp. With each night's lesson and experience, Johnny learns to cope with his illness.

He also learns to relish every aspect of his existence and surroundings. He becomes stronger and wiser with each successive tale. In the final story, Johnny will have almost completely recuperated from his disease.

· · · · · · ·

There are seven episodes in Harry's Stories - the Road to Recovery.

The stories are written in a style that young children and older people will all find easy to follow. The sprinkling of magic throughout gives an enchanting quality. Each story is very easily understood and the healing will subliminally seep through to the reader or listener.

As well as helping the sickly child and elder co-readers or narrators come to terms with illness, the stories are intended to help people develop a Positive Mental Attitude and learn how to enjoy life more (regardless of their transient challenges, no matter how daunting their circumstances may appear at first).

Harry's STORIES

The road to Recovery

Stories to help make children feel better by Alexander Gunningham

Book 1

Harry's Hijinks

Chapter 1

HARRY'S HIGHJINKS

"Beep, beep!" said Harry gently. Gently, but still loud enough to wake up Johnny.

"Beep, beep!" he repeated. "It's time to go for a ride in my car."

Johnny yawned slowly and stared sleepily into the eyes of Harry Bear, who he was clutching in his arms. They were both warm and safe in Johnny's bed in the house where they lived with Mummy and Daddy.

"Where's your car, Harry? I didn't know you had one."

"It's a magic car" Harry replied. "We can only find it in our dreams. Go back to sleep and we'll go for a ride…"

Harry's voice grew softer and was replaced by a soothing tone, half formed of whistle and wind.

Johnny's eyes blinked once, then twice and he was asleep once more.

Harry's paw took Johnny by the hand and they flew together, through a glorious sunlit morning, up to the top of a tall pedestal.

On top of the rocky crag, way above the leafy treetops and the green fields below, was Harry's car. It was multicoloured and very shiny.

The steering wheel and controls were in front of the drivers seat, which was a perfect fit for Harry.

Behind this was another seat which, as luck would have it, was a perfect fit for Johnny. The only difference between the two seats was that Johnny's was much larger than Harry's. But, of course, Johnny was much larger than Harry was. So that was a perfect start.

"Where can we drive up here? There's nowhere to go, surely?", Johnny inquired.

"We go up, up and away!" Harry replied, his voice rising higher with each word like a recorder scale.

"But how? We'll fall out of the sky like a stone. We'll hurt ourselves!" Johnny squawked, sounding like an old crow coughing on a beakful of its own feathers.

"Don't worry", said Harry, turning around and soothingly patting Johnny's hand with his paw, "This is a magic car. We can fly. We'll be quite safe. You'll always be safe with a bear. That's why Mummy and Daddy let you play with me. I'm a magic bear and this is my magic car."

As Harry spoke, the magic car rose slowly into the air. So slowly, that Johnny didn't even notice that they were rising straight up into the air. He only noticed that they'd risen to a higher level when the clouds surrounded them.

The fluffy white clouds surrounded the car and its passengers. Inside, it was warm and dry. Harry unfolded a brightly painted fan which had had been lying on the cars dashboard. When the semi-circle of the fan was completely opened, it looked just like a proud peacocks feathers.

Harry winked at Johnny and said "Watch this! You'll like this trick!" He waved the fan frantically at the clouds, making a large hole in them around the car. "Not only is this a fan, but it's also a magic wand. Look!"

He folded the fan, tapped it on the side of the car and it turned into a wand. Not just any old wand, mind you, but a magic wand. Harry waved the wand in the air above their heads. All sorts of different coloured sparks shot from the wands tip. Red sparks. Orange sparks. Yellow ones. Glowing greens. Bold blues. Illuminated indigos. And, finally, some very vivid violets. Shimmering sparks of every colour of the rainbow flew out of the end of the wand. And with each spark came a loud, fizzing pop.

The sparks became lights that seemed to chase each other in a merry dance. They swirled and shimmied so quickly that they swelled in size until the lights became very large and bright. Around and around spun the lights, quicker and quicker, until Johnny began to feel dizzy. Harry sensed this and, to make Johnny feel better, said "Don't worry. The first stage is almost over. It'll soon settle down and you won't feel giddy. Just relax and breathe slowly and deeply for a little while".

Johnny did as Harry suggested and very soon he did feel better. You can always rely on a bear for comfort, Johnny reassured himself.

In the short time that he'd taken to make himself feel better, which he'd done all by himself, Johnny noticed that the lights had slowed down. They weren't moving as fast and now seemed to be more solid.

"Do you know what it is yet?", Harry asked excitedly.

"Well…it looks like a rainbow, but it's the wrong shape." answered Johnny, scratching his head in his confusion.

"Who says it's the wrong shape? Is there a rulebook for rainbows? Why should rainbows have to be round? I thought you might like to see a straight one, so here it is." Harry leaned his elbow on the armrest of the car, and let a proud smile spread over his face. He took pride in a job well done, which was only right and proper.

Far, far below them came the sounds of many voices gasping with surprise. The surprise then turned to squeals of excitement. Unable to contain themselves, the audience beneath the magnificent unbending rainbow clapped and yelled with delight.

"See? See? They like it. They know good magic when they see it.", Harry said gently.

"But who's down there? I didn't notice anyone before." Johnny asked, peering below. They were so high up, in the middle of the clouds, that he couldn't see who was making all the fuss. He had a good, long look at the landscape below them. No-one was to be seen, but Johnny could hear them all right.

"They're my friends. Most of them live in Happy Valley. Some of them are from the Magic Wood. Others have homes on Heavenly Hill. Would you like to meet them?", suggested Harry.

Johnny nodded his head, too excited to speak. He was sure that a magic bear like Harry would have very special friends.

Harry sang like an early morning bird and waved his magic wand. The rainbow widened, softened, and its angle changed. Instead of standing up straight like a lamp-post, the rainbow now curved. It now looked like an upside down rainbow, which is exactly what it was.

"Hold on tight! We're going down to meet my pals!" shouted Harry above the rush of the wind that swirled about them as the magic car rolled smoothly down the rainbow bridge.

Johnny whooped excitedly. This ride was the most fun that he'd had in ages. It was the most fun that he'd had since his illness had kept him in bed. He began to feel better already. He forgot his health, for the first time in a long while, and savoured every moment of the experience.

As they got closer to the ground, Johnny could see the world below them a lot more clearly. The silver and green waters of the River Glee shone in the warm sunlight as it twisted and turned its merry way through Happy Valley. To the left of the rainbow bridge, stood the green and blue leaved oak trees of the Chuckling Copse.

Beyond them were the tall figures of the silver birch trees of Knowing Wood, leading to the dense thickness of the Magic Wood.

On the right of the rainbow bridge rose the heights of Heavenly Hill. On its slopes the golden sails of the Wishing Windmill sparkled as they turned slowly in the gentle breeze. The Laughing Lighthouse chortled softly to itself, looking forward to its next night-time task of lighting up the Happy Valley dance. Other buildings, on the hillside and valley below, grew larger and larger as they approached the rainbows end.

As the car glided to the foot of the rainbow, Harry triumphantly tooted his cars horn before it stopped in the centre of Harry's friends. Johnny was astonished by the eager crowd that gathered around them. He'd never seen so many bears in his life!

There were big bears and little bears. Fat bears and thinner bears. Tall ones and short ones. Bears of every colour and colour combination (including black, white and many fetching shades of grey).

The tallest of the grey bears, who appeared to be the spokesbear for the group, was as tall as Johnny was. Harry hugged this grey bear warmly, for bearhugs are never cold, and they were clearly old friends.

"Allow me to introduce you…Johnny, this is Porridge… Porridge, this is Johnny." Harry, bowed and spread his arms wide as he introduced his two friends to each other.

Johnny and Porridge shook hand with paw formally, just as Johnny had seen his Daddy do when meeting people that Daddy knew through his work when they were out shopping in the town centre.

"How do you do?", said Johnny and Porridge at the exactly the same moment, which made them both laugh. All the other bears laughed too, pleased that their friend Harry had brought his best friend Johnny to meet them all.

A very pretty red-furred bear, wearing a white dress with a yellow floral pattern, stepped forward and curtsied before Johnny. Johnny, in turn, bowed to her. Porridge spoke for her, as she was a very shy little bear indeed.

"Meet Red, Johnny. She's been working hard all morning, making you a present."

Red stepped forward timidly to approach Johnny. He felt that she was blushing and that her fur had gone a deeper shade of scarlet, but it was impossible to know for certain. "P-p-p-please…" stammered Red nervously, as she always did until she knew somebody a little better, "P-please lower your h-head for a second…"

Johnny did as he was told, knowing that he could trust a bear not to hurt him, and Red placed a garland of blue flowers around his neck. They were the most beautiful flowers Johnny had ever seen in his life. Their perfume was both sweet and powerful. As he breathed in the scent deeply, he felt a warm tingle of well-being spreading all over him. This powerful sensation reached every part of Johnny, from his head to his toes.

"Thank you very much, Red, for such a lovely present.", said Johnny, hurriedly remembering his manners after his initial surprise. "I feel much better wearing these… but how is that possible?"

"They're magic flowers," replied Red, losing her shyness and her stammer now that she was glad that Johnny had appreciated her gift, "They'll stay with you always, but sometimes you won't be able to see them. To everybody else, like your Mummy, Daddy, the doctors and nurses, they'll be invisible. But they'll still be with you, and they'll help you to feel better and help you. They're yours for life. If ever an illness should make you feel sad, remember these blue flowers and you'll feel a little better straight away."

"Thanks again", said Johnny, as a single tear fell from each eye and rolled slowly down his face.

They were tears of relief. He knew that he was going to be strong now. Strong enough to cope.

The bears sensed this and cheered and clapped. They were proud of Johnny and glad that he was determined to get better.

Harry jumped into Johnny's arms. Johnny hugged Harry and held him close to his chest. "It's time for us to go home now." said Harry. "Back to see Mummy and Daddy. Just close your eyes, count backwards from ten down to one and we'll be there."

Johnny did as he was told, for he knew now that Harry was a very special friend that he could trust. In his thoughts he counted backwards.

Ten, nine, eight…the other bears cheering and singing grew fainter in Johnny's ears…seven, six, five…Johnny felt good to be alive…four, three, two…Johnny almost felt brand new…one and awake.

Johnny opened his eyes slowly, and felt Harry's warm fur close to his chest. Harry winked at Johnny and in a whisper, so that no-body else could hear, told him "We'll go back to Happy Valley tonight again and meet the other bears. You'll have to excuse me now, but I'm very tired. I'm going to sleep now and I'll take you back for some more magic tonight. The other bears will be waiting for us and we'll have some fun together. We'll play together just as you did with the other children before you became ill. Now be a brave little boy…Mummy and Daddy are about to bring you your breakfast."

Right at that moment, Mummy and Daddy entered Johnny's bedroom with his breakfast tray. Johnny smiled bravely at his parents, which made them all feel so much better.

Mummy, Daddy and Johnny told each other how much they all loved one another. They shared a gentle group hug together. Outside, in the green apple tree in the garden outside Johnny's bedroom window, a robin redbreast sang its song of thanks and joy. It was another beautiful day, despite the heavy rain and the blustering wind, and it was good to be alive.

Stories to help make children feel better by Alexander Gunningham

Book 2

The Wishing Windmill

Chapter 2

THE WISHING WINDMILL

Johnny had had a wonderful day, despite his still feeling unwell because of his illness. The Doctor had praised him for his new-found outlook on life. Mummy and Daddy had told him how proud they were of him for being so brave.

Even Harry looked pleased. But, then again, he always had a smile on his face. So he always looked pleased. Johnny smiled as he thought that and decided that he wanted to try and be happy all the time. Just like Harry. When the Doctor had told Johnny that he was bearing up very well, Johnny laughed and laughed. Yes, Johnny was up like a bear, all right. And as happy as Harry.

Johnny discovered that being happy was enormously helpful. Every mouthful of his food tasted better. In fact, it tasted delicious. Johnny savoured every mouthful. He also found that his orange juice was more refreshing. The Doctor had said that Johnny had to drink lots of water and, for the first time, this didn't seem so much like hard work. It even seemed to be fun.

Even taking his medicine didn't feel half as bad. Johnny reminded himself that the Doctor had given him the medicine to make him better. He now looked forward to taking his medicine. After all, it was going to make him better.

For the first time in weeks, Johnny had felt strong enough to read some of his favourite stories out loud to Harry. Johnny had always enjoyed this, but now it seemed even better. It was his way of thanking Harry for all the help and support that the loyal bear had given him. How the two friends enjoyed reading together. Johnny enjoyed using different voices for the different people in the stories. Harry seemed to smile more brightly because Johnny was having such fun reading to him.

The day seemed shorter, too. Instead of being bored with lying in bed all day, the time flew past. Johnny enjoyed every second of every minute of every hour of the day. Thanks to Harry, his magic bear, he'd learnt to love life again. And life tasted great.

After Mummy had tucked up Johnny in bed for sleep-time (Johnny didn't have a set bed-time any more because, of course, he had to spend all day in bed). Daddy read Johnny a very funny story from a new book that he'd bought on his way home from work. Johnny had laughed at all the funny parts in the story and Harry's smile seemed to get bigger and bigger.

When the story was over, Mummy and Daddy both kissed Johnny good-night. They turned Johnny's bed-side light off and tip-toed out of the room. For they could see that Johnny was very tired, but also very happy.

It didn't take Johnny long to fall asleep. And he was off to his dreams. Off to Happy Valley with the bears. And there he was. Standing in front of the Wishing Windmill, perched halfway up the Heavenly Hill.

But where was Harry?

"Here I am, Johnny!" called Harry from an open window in the red and yellow brick wall of the Wishing Windmill. "Come inside and see who's waiting for you. Your new friends are here. But first you have to find the way inside. You like playing Hide and Seek with the other children, so you'll like this game too."

With a cheery wave, Harry disappeared inside the Wishing Windmill.

Johnny felt a little scared. This was the first time that he'd been in Happy Valley on his own. But, before he could make himself too upset, three windows magically appeared in the Wishing Windmill's walls above him. They appeared magically, because they weren't there a few moments ago.

In each of the newly formed windows was a familiar, friendly face. There in the square window, smiling away, was Harry. In a triangular window was Red, wearing a pale blue dress today. She leaned forward and threw a giant ox-eye daisy down to Johnny.

Red sang to new her pal Johnny, no longer shy but a lot more musical, from her lofty position: "Don't forget your blue flowers, they're always round your neck, remember them always, they'll keep you safe from harm." Red pulled her head back through the triangular window, which closed and then vanished (magically, of course).

Johnny looked down at his chest. There were his blue flowers. He hadn't noticed them before, but felt that they'd never been away. He picked up the large yellow and white ox-eye daisy from the green grass at his feet. It winked at him and, in a very high and clear voice, told him: "Put me in the sea of blue, I will help you to see through!"

Without knowing why, Johnny's hands moved the ox-eye daisy up to his chest. The flower then wriggled free from his fingers and joined the blue flowers in the garland around his neck. It wound itself into the chain, settling with its head over Johnny's heart.

Johnny felt calmer and safer. Stronger, too. Then he remembered the round window. He looked up to see who was there.

There, sharing a strawberry and mint ice-cream cone with two bears that Johnny hadn't seen before, was Porridge. Porridge and the other two bears were all wearing party hats. "Once you've worked out how to get inside, we'll show you how the Wishing Windmill works". Then, amid much merriment, the three bears vanished inside the round window which closed behind them and vanished. There's magical, thought Johnny, who was getting used to how things worked in Happy Valley.

He looked up at the window where Harry had been, but that had gone too. So he walked around the circular wall of the Wishing Windmill, to try and find a way inside and join his chums at the party.

Johnny walked all the way around the outside of the Wishing Windmill, but there did not seem to be a way inside. He walked around again, this time looking at the top of the building. But there was nothing there to help. No ladder or any other way in. Just the slowly turning golden sails of the Wishing Windmill, creaking gently in the warm afternoon sun.

Having found that there was no way in, Johnny looked around for someone friendly to help. But no-one was in sight. "I wish I knew the way inside!" said Johnny loudly, feeling a little tearful. As soon as he spoke, a large green wooden double door appeared right in front of him. Both halves of the door creaked loudly as they slowly opened towards Johnny.

From within the Wishing Windmill came lots and lots of bears. They were playing musical instruments and marching in step, reminding Johnny of a trip he'd had to London with Mummy and Daddy to see the Changing of the Guard.

Some of the bears were banging on drums. Others were playing flutes. More were blowing shiny brass and silver horns. Harry led the parade, swinging a copper coloured trumpet high in the air as he played it.

"Well done!" shouted Harry above the loud music from the band of bears, "You've cracked the secret! That's how everybody gets in to the Wishing Windmill. Just wish it and you're there."

"That's right." said Porridge, laying down his drum and sticks on the grass. "But you have to be very careful what you wish for at all times, for it might come true. Isn't that right?" The other bears all nodded in agreement. They'd all stopped playing their instruments and had sat down on the ground behind Porridge. They reminded Johnny of his classmates at school, the way that they respected Porridge and were quiet when their teacher spoke.

"Before you go inside the Wishing Windmill, I want you to promise me that you won't wish for anything for yourself other than good health. Because that's all matters in life. Your good health. And…" Porridge paused for effect, "You must also promise not to wish for anything that will cause harm to anybody else. If you promise us that you won't do either of those things, you're very welcome in the Wishing Windmill. Agreed?"

Johnny nodded his head. "I promise, Porridge. I won't let you or the other bears down."

Porridge smiled and added "Don't let Mummy or Daddy down either. Or anybody else. But especially yourself. Always be true. Especially to yourself." Then Porridge put a kindly paw around Johnny's shoulder and they went inside the Wishing Windmill, followed by the other bears.

Inside, it was very dark. Johnny couldn't see anything in front of him. "I wish it was lighter in here", said Johnny out loud. And lighter it was. The walls were covered in moving colours and shapes that changed every few seconds. But it wasn't possible to see what the odd shaped colours, or the odd coloured shapes, were meant to mean. "What a strange sight!" said Johnny to the bears, who were sat in chairs all around the circular wall of the inside of the Wishing Windmill. "If only they meant something . I wish something would help me understand what all this means".

Then the shapes and colours shifted, showing Johnny properly formed pictures. They were moving pictures, just like the ones on television, but clearer and sharper. They also seemed to be solid. The picture on the walls, covering the whole of each wall from top to bottom, was of a garden. The garden had tall trees, pretty flowers, singing birds and above it all (right up high near the ceiling of the Wishing Windmill) was a clear blue sky.

But it wasn't just any garden. "That's our garden!" shouted Johnny excitedly. "That's the garden of the house where I live with Mummy, Daddy and Harry. But how can that be?"

"Well, Johnny", Porridge started to explain as he sat in the biggest chair of them all, "That's because, when you came inside the Wishing Windmill, you wished for happier times. You'll see some happier times in a minute but, before we do, I want to remind you to be careful what you wish for. Because it might come true, and it always will inside the Wishing Windmill.",said Porridge very softly and gently.

Johnny nodded his head silently and eagerly, wanting to show Porridge and the other bears that he was clever enough to understand. "Just enjoy the show. And don't make any more wishes. We're all only allowed a few wishes, so don't waste them. Here are some happier times for you to enjoy." Porridge swept his arm out towards the gently moving pictures on the walls. He did that just like the Ringmaster in the Circus, thought Johnny to himself.

On the walls, Johnny saw a much larger version of himself run into the centre of the garden. He was healthy and happy and enjoying the warm sunshine. Then Mummy and Daddy appeared and they were much bigger, too. Mummy was carrying a tray of glasses and a big jug of Johnny's favourite drink, homemade lemonade.

Johnny could see the yellow drink in the jug shining in the sunlight. He could smell it, too. His favourite smell of sweet lemonade filled the room and made Johnny feel thirstier than he'd ever felt before. Mummy poured a glass of lemonade for the larger Johnny on the wall. Johnny heard himself thanking Mummy for the drink and saw himself take a big gulp of his favourite drink.

"I wish the real Johnny had a glass of lemonade.", said Red, wiping a tear from the scarlet fur just below her right eye. And then she handed a glass to Johnny. It was full of lemonade, which tasted just as good as the lemonade that Mummy made.

Then, on the walls, the giant Daddy reached up to the green leaved lower branches of the apple tree. He plucked a large red ripe apple from the tree, then handed it to the Johnny on the wall. Johnny felt a friendly paw tap him on the shoulder. He turned around and saw Harry standing there, holding out a rosy red apple to Johnny with both paws.

Johnny took the apple gratefully from Harry, thanked him, and sank his teeth into it. It tasted better and sweeter than any apple that he'd eaten before.

"You see, happy days have been and gone. But happy days will always return.", said Porridge, sitting sideways in his chair and gazing up thoughtfully at the violet clouds passing slowly across the blue sky of the Wishing Windmill's ceiling.

"Any day can be a happy day, if you want to make it happen." Porridge stroked the grey fur at the end of his chin before continuing. "If you remember that, you'll be OK. Don't worry about being ill or things that you can't change that day. Just live for the moment and be happy. Tomorrow's another day."

Then the happy picture of Johnny having a good time with Mummy and Daddy faded. The walls turned white and the Wishing Windmill was bathed in silver light. This is just like leaving the cinema after a film, when they turn the lights back on, thought Johnny to himself.

Just like the previous night, Harry hopped up into Johnny's arms. "Remember, count backwards from ten down!" called Harry as the ceiling of the Wishing Windmill opened.

Harry led Johnny, hand in paw, and they flew slowly up through the ceiling. Below them, they heard the band of bears playing music to help them on their way.

Ten, nine, eight…mustn't get myself in a state…seven, six, five, four…I'm so glad I found that door…three, two, one…this is how it's done.

Johnny woke up, with Harry in his arms. It was morning once more and he was back home in bed. On the window ledge of his bedroom, came three gentle taps from the robin redbreast that lived in the apple tree outside. Johnny smiled a smile nearly as wide as Harry's.

It was another fantastic day and Johnny was going to make the most of it.

Harry's Stories
The road to Recovery

Stories to help make children feel better by Alexander Gunningham

Book 3

Jack O' The Red and Green

Chapter 3

JACK O' THE RED AND GREEN

It had been another day of progress. Johnny had been allowed to sit in an armchair by his bedroom window for almost an hour. It was the first time that he'd been out of bed for that long in weeks.

He'd sat there, wrapped up tight in his dressing gown, and watched life outside in the garden. He'd watched lots of birds, flying high above the green lawns before resting on the brown painted fences. The ginger cat from next door had put on a show, too. It had raced up and down the path, dived into the bushes and writhed on its back in the flower beds.

Johnny had laughed at the cats wild behaviour and had wanted to be outside in the garden. He really missed feeling the wind blowing in his hair and even having raindrops falling on his face.

Still, he had kept promising himself, it wouldn't be for long. When he was better, he'd be allowed back into the garden to play. So he didn't mind when Mummy told him to get back into bed. In fact, the short time away had made the bed more comfortable. It didn't feel as though he'd been there for ever, as it had done recently.

It also seemed to make the day shorter. Johnny was quite surprised that sleep-time had come around so soon. He yawned slowly and picked up Harry from the chair by the bed. His friend winked at Johnny, glad to be part of another adventure together.

After Mummy and Daddy had said goodnight to Johnny, Harry leaned over in the bed and whispered in Johnny's ear. "It's time to go back to Happy Valley. Hold on tight!"

Johnny's bed had turned into a red and green coloured hovercraft. Silently, the hovercraft rose above the carpet in Johnny's bedroom. The walls shimmered and changed colour from blue to green. The walls were moving forwards and backwards, in and out, with a gentle breathing sound. The walls seemed to close in around the hovercraft and then they disappeared.

Underneath the hovercraft, in all directions, were the bubbling waters of the River Glee. To their right, the two friends saw the Wishing Windmill on the middle slopes of Heavenly Hill. Underneath the Wishing Windmill's sails, which reflected the sunlight back on to the surface of the water, stood a large cannon. Next to the cannons fuse stood Porridge, holding up little Red. The tiny bear held a lit taper to the fuse.

As the flame lit the fuse, a red cloud of smoke exploded from the other end of the cannon. The sound echoed all around Happy Valley. Just as the sound finally died away, the cannon exploded again. This time, the smoke was green and it flew out of the end of the cannon in rings.

The green smoke rings rose in the air and mingled with the red smoke still hanging in the air. Together they formed a gigantic human face, hanging in mid-air without a body. A booming voice called down towards the two companions in the hovercraft, "Harry…Johnny… I'm over here…" The voice changed to a cackling laugh as the outsized head revolved quickly, before spinning off in the sky towards the woodlands.

"What was that?", Johnny spluttered.

"That's another friend", answered Harry, "We'll be meeting him shortly. But let's get off the river first."

The hovercraft silently swung to the left and away from the water. Once it was away from the riverbank, the hovercraft landed on the grass. Harry hopped out first and started to run up the gentle slope to the trees above. The ever-smiling bear turned to Johnny, who was climbing slowly out of the hovercraft.

"Come on, slowcoach!", cried Harry, "We've got lots to do today." Johnny quickened his step until he caught Harry up.

"Where are we going, Harry?" asked Johnny.

"Lots of places. First, this is the Chuckling Copse.", answered Harry, spreading his arms wide and turning slowly in a circle under the trees. What a funny name, thought Johnny to himself. He was about to ask Harry how the Chuckling Copse got its name, when it became obvious.

The largest of the oak trees in the centre of the Chuckling Copse started sniggering. Its main boughs on either side of the trunk moved just like the arms on a boy or a bear. As the trees laughter grew louder and more frenzied, its boughs clutched the sides of its trunk. It rocked from side to side, whilst staying firmly rooted, as its laughter became ever more louder and higher pitched. The other trees started to join in, until they were all swaying in hysterical harmony.

Harry and Johnny joined in the laughter too. It was impossible not to, because the trees had a very infectious way of laughing. Johnny laughed and laughed until he was sure that he was going to split his sides. Like the trees, he held his hands to his tummy as he laughed. His eyes streamed with tears of happiness, although he wasn't really sure why.

"Feels better already, doesn't it?" said Harry, as he gasped for his breath after all the laughing. "Laughter will always make you feel better. If you try and be happy always, and I know that it can be hard at times, life will be easier and more enjoyable. Just remember the Chuckling Copse when times are hard, you'll soon feel better."

Harry took Johnny's hand in his paw and led him up towards the Knowing Wood. The silver birch trees swayed gently in the breeze and, as the wind blew through the upper branches, they seemed to whisper softly. Johnny turned around slowly in amazement. He'd never seen such trees before. Then Harry magically produced a dustpan and brush, with which he swept up the fallen needles that had fallen off the tree above. He sat down on the floor at the base of the trunk and patted the ground next to him.

"Sit down here. I'll show you how to tune in to the tree. Then you can find out the secrets of the Knowing Wood for yourself.", said the still grinning bear. "Just settle down, calm your mind and clear it of all other thoughts. Let the trees of the Knowing Wood speak to you."

Johnny did as he was told. The trees did speak to him, but not out loud. He felt that all kinds of secrets were being passed on to him by the trees. But not by using words or sounds. It just felt as if he was receiving a lesson by a secret method. "Try it out for yourself.", suggested Harry, "Ask yourself a question and the trees will help you find the answer."

Having closed his eyes, Johnny did as he was told. He was going to make a full recovery from his illness, he was told, but not today. Later on, he was going to have an egg with toast soldiers for breakfast. It would rain in the afternoon. Daddy would moan about his train being late on his way back home from work. Johnny was told all of this and more. Much more. His head reeled with all the things that the trees were telling him.

"Try something else, away from our home. Something that hasn't made sense to you before.", suggested Harry.

Johnny opened his eyes, while he thought of what to ask the trees. He looked up at the sky above. A small cloud passing overhead gave him the idea of what to ask. The trees told him, again silently and without words, all about clouds and rainfall. They told Johnny all kinds of things about the weather and much more besides. He understood everything, he felt. All thanks to the trees and their silent teachings.

"When you are fit enough to go back to school," said Harry, "You'll be able to understand a lot more in your lessons. If you don't understand something in future, come back here and ask for help. It works every time."

Johnny knew exactly what Harry meant, thanks to the trees. He could either come back to the Knowing Wood in his dreams or his daydreams. Then all would become clear, because of the Knowing Wood.

"But there's one last part of the woods that we haven't visited yet.", said Harry, as he stood up. Johnny rose too and together they set off up the hill. Johnny knew that they were heading towards the middle of the Magic Wood. He knew this because the trees of the Knowing Wood had told him so.

He also knew that Harry had left him alone for a while. But Johnny wasn't worried or scared. He knew that it was just another test for him, to help him cope better. So he felt quite relaxed and at ease as he climbed the hill towards the Magic Wood. Even the change in the weather didn't worry Johnny. The air felt very cold all around him and heavy rain and hailstones as big as apples began to fall on the hillside. Loud thunder sounded as blue streaks of forked lightning pierced through the suddenly dark sky.

But with each further step, Johnny felt a little short of breath. He also felt his legs and shoulders get heavier. His whole body began to get slower and he started sweating. As he sank to his knees on the green grass, Johnny asked himself what was happening. He was just about to give up on his journey, which now seemed impossible to carry on with, when he remembered the Knowing Wood.

He decided to ask the trees of the Knowing Wood what to do. He knew the answer right away.

Johnny knew that he had to fly up the last part of the hill. So he did. He stretched his arms out wide, like a bird, and floated high above the ground. He flew to the top of the hill and gently landed beneath a vast old hazel tree. Johnny felt great. All his tiredness had gone and he'd found the flying very easy and very enjoyable. The weather had changed, too. It was now very sunny and the rain and winds had stopped.

He wondered where Harry was and why he was up on top of the hill, all on his own.

"You're never alone in the Knowing Wood.", boomed a very deep but kindly voice above him. Johnny looked up in the direction of the voice. Up above him, squatting in the lower branches of the tree, was an odd looking man. He was dressed in a shirt and trousers which were both covered in broad red and green stripes. On his feet were red and green striped pointed-toe shoes. On his head was a pointed hat, also red and green striped.

Johnny had never seen anyone with such a pointed chin or such a long nose before. He was quietly thinking this to himself, when the strange man spoke to him. "You're pretty funny looking yourself, in these parts, young Johnny", said the man in the tree, pointing a long and bony finger at Johnny.

"And the answer to the question that you just thought of is…I am a gnome and my name is Jack o' the Red and Green."

Jack hopped out of the tree and landed in front of Johnny. "I'll help you understand more later. But first we need to have a reminder of what fun is. Ready for a bit of fun, Johnny?"

Johnny nodded his head eagerly. Jack pulled a wand from his belt and waved it in a circle over the grass. From under the soil sprouted some green and red creepers, which forced their way up with a noise like bedsprings being bounced on. The creepers crossed over each other and formed the shape of a trampoline.

"Go on, Johnny, have a go. You'll be quite safe.", said Jack soothingly.

Johnny did as he was told, without any fear. He climbed up onto the surface of the trampoline and gently bounced up and down. He began to worry about bouncing too high and falling off the trampoline.

"Go on, Johnny!", cried a familiar voice. "We'll make sure that you don't fall off!" Johnny looked beyond the edge of the trampoline and saw Harry with all the other bears there. It was just like using the trampoline in the school gymnasium, with all his friends there to stop him falling off and hurting himself.

Sure that he was safe with all the bears there, Johnny jumped higher and higher and higher. He'd never jumped this high on a trampoline before. With each leap he saw more and more of the Magic Wood and Happy Valley below him.

"That's enough for one day, Johnny." , called Jack. As he did so, the trampoline turned into a giant red and green-striped cushion. Johnny landed safely on the cushion.

"One last thing before Harry takes you home. All that flying is all very good but you need to be properly grounded.", said Jack producing a pair of very large red and green-striped boots from behind his back. "These will keep your feet firmly on the ground when you get home."

Jack threw the boots to Johnny. They landed at his feet and, with a loud slurping sound, covered his normal shoes. Johnny now felt very calm, safe and happy.

"Come on or we'll miss breakfast", said Harry, taking Johnny's hand in his paw once again. As Jack and the other bears waved and called their farewells to the pair, a red and green mist grew around them.

Johnny realised that he was back home in bed with Harry again. It was the start of another day and another adventure, he told himself. Harry nodded his head in agreement as he sleepily yawned and stretched.

Harry's Stories
The road to Recovery

Stories to help make children feel better by Alexander Gunningham

Book 4

The Whirlpool

Chapter 4

THE WHIRLPOOL

Johnny was back in hospital. He had felt very poorly and the Doctor had sent him there for more tests. At the hospital, they had told Johnny not to worry. They just wanted to keep him in so that they could watch for any changes in Johnny's condition.

Mummy and Daddy had left Johnny at the end of visiting time. Harry had been left at home. Johnny was all on his own. But he didn't feel sad. He remembered everything that Harry's friends had told him. The words of Porridge and Jack o' the Red and Green made him feel better within himself. When his illness made him feel unwell, he comforted himself with thoughts of his friends in Happy Valley and the Magic Wood.

When the Nurse gave Johnny his medicine, he'd taken it with a cheerful smile. He'd learnt to be positive and to get on with life. He'd also heard a familiar and friendly voice, whispering in his ear.

It was his friend Harry, talking to him by some kind of magic. "Don't worry, everything will be fine.", said Harry soothingly. "I'll come to you in your dreams and we'll have another adventure together. Remember, nothing lasts for ever. So you won't be in hospital for ever, either. I'll see you later." Harry blew Johnny a raspberry, which always made Johnny laugh, and then was silent.

The evening passed slowly and then Johnny fell asleep in the hospital bed. But, in his dreams, Johnny was wide awake. He was falling through black darkness, with his hair being blown by a wind from underneath him. Then the darkness became lighter and changed to an inky blue. Johnny seemed to be falling for a very long time. When was he going to land, he wondered to himself.

"Soon, soon, you'll see!", called a very familiar voice above him. Johnny looked up and saw Harry falling towards him. Johnny caught Harry with both hands and held him close to his chest. "Hold me tight and we'll get out of here!", shouted Harry above the noise of the rushing wind. Then the bear pulled a cord attached to a pack that was strapped to his back.

A multi-coloured parachute sprang out of the pack on Harry's back and billowed in the wind. But, instead of falling slowly to the ground, the pair were swept upwards. Up and up they flew, higher and higher, until the light around them grew paler. It was now as blue as the sky on a warm Summer day. The air around them felt warmer, too.

Johnny held on tightly to Harry, so that he wouldn't fall back into the cold of the darkness again. Johnny noticed some red and green lights, that were spinning around in the sky and getting closer to the two flying friends. The lights spun closer and Johnny saw that they were now closer together. Then the lights formed the body of an old friend. Jack o' the Red and Green was back.

Jack waved a wand of hazel in a circle and made two magical clouds. One was red and the other green. Jack sat on the larger of the two clouds, which was the green one. Harry and Johnny sat on the red cloud, which hovered next to the green one.

"Welcome to the Whirlpool!", said Jack, spreading his hands wide to show that that's where they were, "I'm glad to see that you've learnt your lessons, Johnny. Keep thinking positive thoughts and you'll make it to your journeys end."

Jack then flourished his hazel wand again and aimed it at Johnny. From the end of the wand flew red and green sparks. The sparks circled Johnny's head and Johnny felt a warm and pleasant tingling around his forehead and temples. He reached to feel what had happened to him.

On his head, Johnny found a crown of red and green flowers, which fitted his head perfectly. "Just like the flowers that little Red Bear gave you, they'll stay with you and protect you at all times", said Jack. "They're magic flowers and they'll help you to enjoy yourself at all times. No matter how ill you are or how much pain you're in, they'll help you feel better".

Johnny put the magic crown back on his head. Looking down at his chest, he noticed that the blue flowers that Red had given him were still there. Realising this made Johnny feel better.

"Now I must leave you.", said Jack as he raised his hazel wand once more. "I shall see you in the groves of the Magic Wood later." The magic wand was flourished and the green cloud, with Jack sitting on it, sped quickly upwards. The green cloud got smaller and smaller as it got further away. Then it disappeared altogether, with a loud popping sound.

"I'm off, too.", announced Harry, as his multi-coloured parachute lifted behind him and carried the bear off the red cloud. Once again, Johnny was alone. But, just the same, he felt good.

A loud crackling sound below him made Johnny look under his cloud. Beneath him were rising flames and smoke. Johnny knew that this was another test for him, so he wasn't worried in the slightest. He just took a few deep breathes and set about calming himself. He also decided to try and enjoy himself.

Red flames leapt around him, but Johnny didn't get burnt. He did feel very hot, though, as the flames completely surrounded him. Inside the fire, the flames were orange and yellow. Johnny noticed that he was sweating a lot. He saw other colours in the flames, too. At the edges of the fire, he saw green flames. Looking up above his head, Johnny saw blue and indigo smoke rising from the inferno. Above the smoke was a shimmering violet haze.

The heat was now really uncomfortable, but Johnny was able to cope. He wondered how he was going to escape the raging flames, when he remembered the Knowing Wood. Johnny imagined himself sitting under an old oak tree in the Knowing Wood and asked his question. Straight away, he knew what to do.

Johnny wished for some rain. The water started falling on Johnny and the fire surrounding him. Down it fell, making the heat seem more bearable. The rain was coloured, too. Johnny had wished for some magic rain and that's exactly what he got. Being magic rain, it was all the colours of the rainbow.

Johnny cupped his hands to catch some of the red rain. He then drank some of it. It was strawberry flavoured. Johnny was very thirsty after sitting in the fire and drank the rain quickly. He cupped his hands again in a downpour of orange coloured rain. This was orange flavoured, he discovered. The yellow rain tasted of lemonade. The green rain of limeade. Still very thirsty, Johnny tried the blue rain. It was also delicious and tasted of the plums that grew in the garden of his home. The indigo was blackcurrant tasting. And the violet tasted of the sugared violet sweets that his Grandmother kept for her visitors.

The rain had also put out the flames. Although Johnny was still very hot, he was in less pain. As the rain fell on him, Johnny felt better and better. The cloud beneath him had been swept away by the rain.

Johnny's feet were covered in rainwater. On the surface of the water, he could see shimmering and swirling rainbow patterns. The level of the water quickly rose above Johnny's knees and his waist. Soon it was up to his chest and then his neck. Johnny realised that soon the water would be over his head, but he wasn't worried.

When the water finally did rise above him, Johnny calmly carried on breathing. Unlike his trips to the beach for a swim, he didn't get water up his nose or in his mouth. He just carried on breathing as if he were on dry land.

Flashes of colour and air bubbles swirled all around Johnny. The current became faster and faster and Johnny found himself being spun around in the Whirlpool. Around and around he span, with the Whirlpool getting quicker and quicker. Johnny felt himself being sucked deeper into the Whirlpool. Down he was swept, with the colours of the water around him changing from red to blue.

Johnny kept on being carried down by the Whirlpool, which reminded him of watching the bathwater being sucked down the plug-hole. At the bottom of the Whirlpool was a man-hole cover with a handle. Johnny held onto the handle and tried to pull it out to escape on the other side, but the current was too strong for him. He couldn't shift it and felt his arms getting weaker. Silently, for the Whirlpool was too noisy for him to speak, Johnny wished for help.

Straight away, the cover moved and the Whirlpool moved up and away from Johnny. Inside the hole where the man-hole cover had been was Harry's smiling face. "Come on!", called Harry to his now very tired friend, "There's one last part of the journey. Follow me!"

Johnny did as Harry told him to, despite him aching painfully all over. He climbed through the hole and found himself in a very dark tunnel. He wished he could see where he was going. The magic worked again and the tunnel was lit by some orange stones set in the brown mud wall of the tunnel.

The tunnels light was bright enough for Johnny to feel comfortable about entering, so he did. Ahead of him was Harry, carrying a big black torch in one paw and a coiled yellow rope in the other. Johnny followed Harry, feeling stronger now that he was no longer being pulled about by the force of the Whirlpool.

At first, the tunnel was level. But the further the two friends went, the steeper it became. The orange stones in the tunnel wall now had larger stones shining white-light next to them. It was almost as bright as day in the tunnel.

Ahead of them in the tunnel wall, Johnny saw a much smaller hole with a family of rabbits in it. They were clapping their paws together in encouragement as Harry and Johnny got closer. Beyond the friendly bunnies hole was the end of a tree root, hanging out of the roof of the tunnel above them.

"It's not far now!", squealed Harry excitedly, "We'll soon be there!"

On they went along the tunnel, which was now getting wider. Harry stopped underneath some dangling tree roots. He shone his torch at the tunnels ceiling and Johnny saw that there was a hole in the roof of the tunnel.

Harry whistled a tune and the yellow rope in his paw twitched slightly. Then, as the melody echoed in the tunnel, the rope rose upwards towards the hole. Harry climbed onto the rope, still whistling, and slid up it. Johnny grabbed hold of the rope too. As he did so, he felt himself being dragged upwards by something very strong.

Ahead of him, Johnny could see the light from Harry's torch showing the way. He could smell the mustiness of the woods after a shower of rain. He realised that they were inside a tree trunk.

Then, to the sound of many happily chirruping birds, the friends were out of the tunnel. Together they stood by a hole in the trunk of a tree. They were in front of Jack o' the Red and Green's hazel tree in the Magic Wood.

And there was Jack, standing in the middle of the grove surrounded by a circle of bears. He beckoned the two to come forward and join them. The bears had been enjoying a picnic. Johnny was very hungry after his long journey and was glad that there was still plenty left over for him.

After Johnny had eaten, Jack stood up from his place in the centre of the circle and spoke to Johnny.

"It's time for you to go now", he said, "But we'll meet again soon. You'll find that your journey has made you stronger. We'll all very proud of you and the way that you coped. Well done, Johnny."

The bears all cheered and then they all seemed to wobble and become fuzzy. Johnny blinked a few times to see more clearly.

Looking around him, he saw that he was back in his hospital bed. A nurse sat by the side of the bed smiled at him. "Morning, Johnny!", she said cheerfully. "You were tossing and turning quite a bit in the night and got very hot, too. But your temperature is normal now."

Later on that morning, the Doctor examined Johnny and said that he could go home soon. Johnny smiled and looked forward to seeing his favourite bear again.

Stories to help make children feel better by Alexander Gunningham

Book 5

Porridge's Scooter

Chapter 5

PORRIDGE'S SCOOTER

Johnny was back home from hospital. He was glad to be home again. Mummy and Daddy had made him a special cake, with lit sparklers on the top, and had made him feel very special. Johnny had missed his parents, his books, his toys and, especially, Harry.

The day had passed very quickly. Now it was sleep-time again and Johnny was glad of it. All the excitement of coming home had made him very tired. After Mummy had turned off the light and left him, Johnny reached out to hold Harry. It felt good to have a bear-hug again.

"Close your eyes and go to sleep.", whispered Harry. "It's time to go back to Happy Valley again." Johnny closed his eyes and fell asleep straight away.

Johnny found himself sitting in a very large yellow and purple flower. Next to him, snuffling because of the flowers pollen, was Harry. Johnny peeped over the edge of the flower. The ground was a long way down. The flower began to sway in the breeze. Johnny and Harry were both rocked by the movement. The flower moved in the wind again and Johnny became a little anxious.

Harry, sensing his friends discomfort, spoke. "Don't worry, I'll get us out of this fix.", said the smiling bear. "All we need is a makeshift parachute. This will do." Harry reached out and pulled a petal from the flower. He chose one that was about to fall off the flower. "Hold me tight." Instructed Harry, holding the purple petal above his head.

Johnny did as he was told and, just as he'd got a firm grip around Harry's waist, the breeze carried the pair up and out of the flower. Together they gently floated down to the green grass below. After they'd landed, Johnny looked around. He felt sure that they were in Happy Valley, but didn't know where.

They were sitting in a grassy hollow that was shaped like a bowl. Johnny looked up at the flower that they'd just left. It was very tall and much higher than the trees that Johnny was used to seeing. Then he heard some voices singing. Johnny knew the voices. It was little Red and Porridge. But where were they? All Johnny could see, apart from Harry and the very tall flower, was the edge of the grass bowl.

Then, over the top of the grass bowl, sped a silver scooter. Riding the scooter were Red and Porridge with a few other bears. They stopped in front of Johnny and Harry. After a few friendly bear-hugs all round, Porridge spoke. "Welcome back to Happy Valley! Hop on the scooter and we'll go for a ride. This scooter's really quick."

Excitedly, Johnny and Harry joined the other bears on the scooter. It carried them up to the edge of the grass bowl and down the steep hill on the other side. The faster the scooter went, the bears made more noise. They squawked and whooped their delight as the two-wheeler shot down the hillside.

"Hold on tight, Johnny!", shouted Porridge over the noise of the other bears. Johnny gripped the handlebars tightly and felt the wind blowing in his face. It seemed to blow away the stuffiness of the hospital. Johnny hadn't felt this good or had as much fun in ages.

At the bottom of the hill was the foot of another hill of blue grass. Instead of stopping, the silver scooter kept going up the second hill. The two-wheeler got faster as it climbed the hill. Johnny noticed that neither he, Porridge or any of the other bears had been using their feet or paws to make the scooter keep going. Of course, Johnny thought to himself, it's a magic scooter.

They were getting still faster as they reached the top of the hill. Johnny expected the scooter to either stop or to go down the other side of the hill. But, instead, it took off and they were flying. Flying high above Happy Valley and the twists and turns of the River Glee below them.

Johnny felt the wind in his hair. It felt good after all that time spent indoors.

The scooter circled the Wishing Windmill, just missing its golden sails (which made all the bears squeal loudly). Then the scooter landed on top of a Clock Tower that Johnny didn't remember being in Happy Valley. "Follow me, everybody!", shouted Porridge. The large grey bear opened a hatch in the flat roof of the clock tower and jumped down into the darkness inside. One by one, the other bears followed Porridge.

Then only Harry and Johnny were left on the roof of the Clock Tower. "What about the magic scooter?", asked Johnny. "Don't worry," replied Harry, "It'll be quite safe up here. Porridge always parks it on the roof. Let's go down and join the others."

Then Harry, too, dived into the hatch on the roof of the Clock Tower and disappeared. Johnny jumped after him. He wasn't scared, because he knew that the bears wouldn't let him come to any harm.

Inside the Clock Tower, there was bright light. Johnny saw a red and yellow striped helter-skelter. Below him were the bears, sliding down and cheering loudly and excitedly. Johnny jumped onto the helter-skelter and slid down the spirals.

At the bottom of the spiral was a big green and white polka-dot cushion. Johnny landed on it safely and it broke his fall. He stood up and looked around at the walls inside the Clock Tower. They were covered with different clocks of different sizes. Big clocks, little clocks, clocks going backwards and others forwards. Some clocks had stopped and others were winding themselves with keys. Most of the clocks were loudly tick-tocking and a few were cuckooing too.

Johnny began to feel a little dizzy looking up at all the clocks. Porridge spoke up above all the noise from the busy clocks. "All these different clocks are here to remind us that different people and different things move at different speeds and times." This made Johnny look puzzled, so Porridge carried on, " Just like your illness. You'll recover faster than some children and slower than others. Some children will seem to be sick for ever, others will be better in what seems like no time. But, fast or slow, everyone recovers at the right speed for them."

Johnny nodded his head, to show that he understood the words of the wise old bear. "And now it's time to leave the Clock Tower.", said Porridge, leading the way through a door. Not just any old door, mind you, but a magic door.

The door was shimmering with a blue light and made a loud buzzing sound. As Johnny stepped through the door, he noticed something very strange. On the side that he'd just left, it had been very warm and sunny. But on the other side, it was cold and dark. There was snow on the ground and a chilly wind blowing. Johnny shivered and hugged himself, rubbing his upper arms to try and get warmer.

Porridge answered Johnny's question before he'd had a chance to ask it. "We're deep in the heart of Midwinter Wood.", he explained. "It's always Winter here and always cold. But life goes on, as it always does."

Johnny turned around slowly in the snow and looked at their surroundings. They were in a grove of trees, whose branches were all bare. There was not a single leaf on any of the trees in the grove. Johnny listened closely. He could hear the trees sighing, as if they were tired. He could also hear the creaking of the trees branches.

"These trees are resting, because they know that it's Winter.", said Porridge. "When they're fully rested, they can move on again to Springtime. In Spring, they can grow leaves again and stand tall once again. They know that it's Winter, and they can feel the cold, but it doesn't worry them. They know that Spring always follows Winter. Just as you should remember that, although you're ill today, you will get better."

Johnny nodded his head again, to show Porridge that he understood what he was being told. He also felt a little better for having things explained.

"There's someone else that I'd like you to meet.", said Porridge, waving a magic wand made of red and green wood. Gold and silver sparks flew out of the end of the wand. The sparks flew up towards the sky. Suddenly there was a flash of blue light above them.

Johnny saw a beautiful lady floating in the sky above. She wore a long white dress and had large wings on her back. But the wings didn't flap like a birds wings, they just lay flat behind her. On her head was a crown of clear white jewels, which flashed with red and blue lights.

She floated down to join Johnny and the bears, hovering just above the snow covered ground. She introduced herself. "I'm Flora. I'm a friend of Jack o' the Red and Green. He's told me what a brave boy you've been.", she said with a smile. Johnny felt himself blushing, but was still pleased to get a compliment.

"It's time for Midwinter Wood to change.", Flora continued. "It's time for it to become…Springtime Wood." She puffed out her cheeks and blew out a line of little green and gold flying stars from her mouth. The tiny stars flew all around the grove. Each one landed on a different tree.

The trees made loud creaking noises as they stretched their limbs. Some of them seemed to yawn as they stretched their branches. Johnny joined in with the stretching, although he wasn't sure why. He felt the muscles in his arms and legs become less stiff and sore as he moved them. Flora looked pleased that Johnny had joined the trees in their exercises.

Johnny noticed that the trees, which had been drooping, were now standing tall and proud. He also noticed lots of little green buds appear on their branches. These buds quickly turned into green leaves. White flowers grew out of the clusters of leaves on the trees.

The air was much warmer, too. Johnny saw the snow melt and turn into little streams of water, which ran down the hill away from the grove. Down at his feet appeared all sorts of pretty flowers. Bluebells, daisies and buttercups popped up all over the wood.

Birds were singing in every tree. Johnny saw some squirrels emerge from under a bush and playfully chase each other across the treetops. Yellow and blue butterflies flew around the petals of the flowers. Spring was back and every living thing in the wood seemed happy because of it.

"Remember, Johnny, Spring always follows Winter.", said Flora. "And, most of the time, wellness follows illness. But that will only happen if you want it to. You'll only get better if you really want to." Johnny smiled and all the bears cheered.

"I do want to get better and I will!", said Johnny a little louder than he'd meant to. But he meant what he said.

"Good, good!", said Flora, clapping her hands. "Then you will and everybody can live happily ever after." The bears gave three loud cheers and, holding paws in a circle, danced excitedly around Johnny.

As the bears danced, Johnny felt a cooling breeze blow over him. He noticed that he was no longer sweating, which he'd been trying to forget about for ages.

"It's time for you to go back home now, Johnny.", said Flora. "But you'll be back in Happy Valley soon. So, until the next time…" Flora blew Johnny a kiss, just as his Grandma did when he left her house. But, unlike Grandma's kiss, Flora's kiss was made of blue smoke.

As the blue smoke rings got closer to Johnny, everything in the wood seemed to be wobbling. Johnny blinked his eyes to clear them, but everything was hidden by the blue smoke.

Johnny closed his eyes again and, when he opened them again, found himself back in his bedroom.

It was morning and the birds were singing outside in the garden. Johnny put his hand to his forehead. He was no longer feverish and his temperature seemed to be normal again. Maybe it hadn't been just a dream, after all.

Maybe he was getting better. Maybe Harry knew the answer. But the bear just kept smiling and didn't say a word.

That was good enough for Johnny.

Harry's Stories

The road to Recovery

Stories to help make children feel better by Alexander Gunningham

Book 6

Changes for the Better

Chapter 6

CHANGES FOR THE BETTER

The Doctor had given Johnny some good news. Although he was still ill, he was much better. Johnny had been very pleased to hear this. He felt better too.

He didn't mind quite so much having to be in bed all day. After all, he kept reminding himself, it wouldn't be forever. He looked forward to being able to go outside again. The thought of being able to ride his bike again made him smile. There were so many things that he'd missed doing, but he'd soon be able to do them again.

Thinking these positive thoughts made the day pass very quickly. Every time Johnny felt that he needed cheering up, he looked at Harry. The bears smiling face always made him feel better.

At sleep-time he was very happy. There he was, safely tucked up in bed with Harry to keep him company. Johnny closed his eyes with a smile on his face as broad as Harry's and went to sleep.

He was sitting on a branch of a tall tree. He looked down at the ground below him, which was a long way down. The wind made the branch that Johnny was sitting on bend a little. This scared Johnny a bit and he clutched the branch tightly so that he wouldn't fall. But where was Harry, he thought to himself.

"Here I am!", piped a familiar voice. Johnny looked up and saw Harry swinging on a branch above him, just like the acrobats that he'd seen at the circus.

Harry answered Johnny's next question, before he'd had a chance to ask it. (Such are the ways of magic bears.)

"Don't worry, a friend will come to rescue us. Any second...now!" Just as Harry finished speaking, there was a flash of purple light. At the middle of this light were spinning green and white lights. The lights began to slow down and take a solid form. Flora was back, floating in front of Johnny's branch.

"Welcome back to Happy Valley!", sang Flora. "You do look odd, perched on that branch. Would you like to get off?" Johnny nodded his head, but not too quickly in case the movement made him fall. Flora smiled and waved a magic wand of blue glass.

From the end of Flora's wand shot different coloured feathers. Red feathers that were the colour of a sunset. Canary yellow feathers. Orange ones. Emerald green plumes. Ocean blues. Imperial indigoes. And, finally, some vividly violet down.

The feathers swirled around Johnny like a whirlwind. At first, Johnny coughed and sneezed a lot. But then he stopped. His throat no longer felt dry and tickly. His nose and eyes stopped running. He felt better, but also felt very strange.

Johnny heard Harry laughing above him. "Look at you! You're all covered in feathers. You look just like your Auntie's parrot! Who's a pretty boy, then?"

Johnny looked down at his hands. Or, rather, where his hands had been. Instead, he saw brightly coloured feathered wings. He looked down at his legs. Instead of wearing his pajama trousers, his legs were much thinner and also covered in feathers of every colour.

He began to realise that he'd changed. He'd changed into a bird. Did this mean that he could fly, he asked himself.

"Yes, you can fly.", said Flora, who could read Johnny's thoughts by magic. "All you need is the confidence and a little wind to help you along. Go on, flap your wings and see."

Johnny did as Flora suggested. He flapped his wings as he perched on the branch. He felt himself being lifted up a little. More confidently, he let go of the branch. He waved his wings up and down. He was flying!

Around and around he flew in circles. This was better than riding a bike, Johnny thought to himself. Less bumpy, for a start. As he circled through the treetops, taking care not to fly into any of them, Johnny remembered that he had a voice.

"Look at me, Harry! I'm flying!", squawked Johnny in a strange new voice. He realised that Harry had been right. He not only looked like Auntie's parrot, but he also sounded like it.

A little tired after using his new wings, Johnny settled on the branch next to Harry. It felt good to rest for a few moments.

Harry plucked a magic mirror from the air (by magic, of course). He held it up so that Johnny could see his own reflection. "Who's a pretty boy, then?", laughed Harry.

Johnny looked in the mirror. He saw his own face looking back at himself. But it was a very different face. His nose and mouth had gone and been replaced by a big black beak. His eyes were now black and orange, just like Harry's. His hair had been replaced by many different coloured feathers. Cocking his head to one side, Johnny decided that he didn't look too bad as a bird.

"Right then.", said Johnny in his odd new parroty voice. "Where shall we fly to?"

50

"Follow me.", answered Flora. "I'll show you the way."

Johnny flapped his wings with Harry holding on to his legs. Together they followed Flora, who flew high above the woods and over the green fields below. Johnny was able to fly a little better when he discovered that gliding on the wind was much easier than moving his wings up and down all the time. Being a bird was brilliant, he decided.

Flora soared up to the clouds and Johnny followed, with Harry dangling below him on his legs. They flew through the clouds and up into the clear blue sky above. The wind, which had become a little chilly the higher that they'd flown, became much warmer with the sunlight.

Then, through a break in the clouds below them, Johnny saw the bubbling surface of the River Glee. Flora flew down through the gap in the clouds, with Johnny and Harry just behind her.

Down they flew towards the River Glee, with the wind blowing hard in their faces. Just as they were about to hit the waters of the River Glee, Flora pulled out of the dive. So did Johnny, only a little too late to stop Harry's legs splashing in the water. But Harry didn't mind and he chuckled happily.

Flora hovered over the field next to the riverbank and Johnny let Harry down on to the ground beneath him. The two friends lay on their backs next to each other, laughing happily together.

"A change is as good as a rest, or so they say.", said Flora. "Would you like another change for the better?"

"Oh, yes please!", answered Johnny eagerly.

"Very well.", said Flora, waving another magic wand of red crystal.

A red jet of water flew out of the end of the wand and splattered all over Johnny.

The wave of water was so strong that it swept Johnny into the River Glee. At first, Johnny was worried about getting his fabulous new feathers wet. He looked down where his wings had been. They were gone and so were his legs.

Johnny noticed that he was able to breathe quite easily under the water, which struck him as being very strange. Above the water, he saw Harry leaning over the riverbank and holding out the magic mirror. Johnny swam to the surface and looked closely at his reflection in the mirror.

He'd changed again. He was no longer a bird, but a fish. His eyes were big, round and black. He didn't have a nose or a beak. No hair or feathers either. His skin was covered in silvery scales that shone with every colour of the rainbow. Johnny saw his mouth opening and closing quickly, just like his pet goldfish at home.

Johnny stuck his head out of the water, so that he could hear what Flora was saying to him.

"You need to carry on the next stage of your journey. The River Glee will take you to the Road to Recovery. All you have to do is go with the flow. Don't swim against the tide and you'll get there quicker." Johnny realised that he had been swimming against the flow. He'd had to, just to stop being carried away by the flow of the waters.

Flora flew off in the direction that the River Glee was flowing with Harry running behind her through the green grass by the riverbank.

Johnny went with the flow. He still had to steer from side, because the River Glee had many different twists and turns. Johnny the fish swam to the right and to the left. He bumped his head a couple of times on tree roots that were dangling into the water. He didn't care that he couldn't say "Ouch!", because it didn't really hurt.

He noticed that swimming with the flow was much less tiring than flying as a bird. He began to feel stronger and stronger the further he swam. Sometimes other fishes joined him on his journey. There were big fishes and little fishes. Some were red, some were green and some were blue. The other fishes swam up little streams that fed into the River Glee and disappeared from view, but Johnny stayed on course.

Then, just as Johnny the fish was starting to tire, a magic net blocked the river. Johnny was able to rest against the net, which was soft and strong and looked just like a blue spiders web.

Flora picked Johnny carefully out of the water and tapped him gently with an orange wand that looked as if it was made from barley sugar. She then put Johnny gently on the ground.

Johnny realised that he was no longer a fish. He looked down and saw that he had arms and legs again. But they weren't the same arms and legs that he'd started with. They were covered in blond fur, just like Harry.

Harry, still a little out of breath from all his running, held up the magic mirror for Johnny to see his own reflection. Johnny had changed again. This time, he had changed into a bear. He looked very similar to Harry, only much taller.

Johnny also found that he had a voice. It was much deeper than his normal voice and seemed to be very loud after all that time swimming in silence.

"I'm a bear, just like Harry!", boomed Johnny in his deep new voice.

"That means that I can climb trees, like all the other bears. Come on, Harry, I'll race you."

The two friends ran to the edge of a wood that Johnny hadn't seen before. At the edge of the wood stood a row of Silver Birch trees. Harry picked one Silver Birch to climb and Johnny chose another one next to it. Flora gave them a count of three and the race up the trees began.

Johnny found that climbing trees was much easier as a bear then as a boy. He reached the top of his tree long before Harry did. Then they climbed down slowly, being extra careful not to fall and hurt themselves.

"That was really good!", said Johnny the bear. "I feel so much fitter and stronger as a bear. I feel as though I can do anything!"

"Good!", said Flora, clapping her hands in delight. "Just remember this feeling when you're back at home, away from Happy Valley. Then you will be able to do whatever you want, within reason and with Mummy and Daddy's permission . You've still got to be careful, mind, that you don't do anything that might hurt yourself or others. Will you promise to do that?"

Johnny nodded his head and let out a big bear growl of agreement.

"That's alright, then.", said Flora with a big smile. "You keep your word and I'll show you the Road to Recovery. But not now. Now it's time for you to go home to Mummy and Daddy. I'll see you next time."

She then produced another magic wand, which was black and shiny like a stick of liquorice, and waved it at Johnny and Harry. Everything went black and was then replaced by a brilliant white light.

Johnny was back home in bed again. He looked at the curtains and could see that it was daytime again. Johnny looked down at his hands and saw that they were back to normal. He was a boy again.

He snuggled up to Harry for a bear-hug. He was soon going to be on the Road to Recovery.

He was almost there.

Stories to help make children feel better by Alexander Gunningham

Book 7

The Road to Recovery

Chapter 7

THE ROAD TO RECOVERY

Johnny hadn't had a dream for several nights. He'd been more ill than he had been in a long while and couldn't sleep. He'd also been even more tired than ever before, but had tried not to worry about it.

He remembered what he'd learnt in Happy Valley and smiled as he did so. Although he felt too ill to travel, whether from his bed or in his dreams, he still felt a lot wiser and more grown-up.

The Doctor had thought that Johnny was very ill again and had almost called an Ambulance. But he'd seen how strong and calm and relaxed that Johnny had become and didn't feel that an Ambulance was needed.

So he left Johnny with a few words of encouragement and a promise to see him tomorrow morning. Shortly after the Doctor had left, Johnny fell asleep at last.

Johnny was sitting in a small wooden boat that was moving slowly across a wide river. The river was so wide that Johnny couldn't see the banks at either side. Above him, the sun shone hotly and Johnny found that his pajamas soon became soaked through with sweat.

He wiped his forehead with the sleeve of his pajama jacket to stop the sweat from running into his eyes. Johnny noticed that the boat was moving faster through the water. He could hear a rumbling noise somewhere in front of him, that sounded a bit like thunder.

Shielding his eyes with his hand from the sun, Johnny looked where the boat was heading. In front of the boat, some distance away, was a floating log. The log disappeared. Screwing his eyes up to see better, Johnny realized that he was heading for a waterfall.

He looked at the bottom of the boat for oars or a paddle, but found neither. Johnny tried using his hands as paddles to turn the boat away from the waterfall. This didn't work and the boat moved closer and closer to the edge. Johnny was very scared and realised that, in less than a minute, he and the boat would fall.

Then Johnny heard the sound of trumpets and drums and pipes being played. He looked behind him and saw a big red steamship. Standing on the upper deck were all the bears, playing the instruments. As the steamer pulled alongside Johnny's little boat, Harry jumped into it from the ship and tied a golden rope to the prow (using a bear-knot, which is a very strong knot indeed).

Harry was just in time. Another few seconds and Johnny would have gone over the waterfall. Johnny had never been so glad to see anybody before. He and Harry shared a quick bear-hug as the red steamship turned around and away from the waterfall. As Johnny's little boat was towed to safety, the band of bears carried on playing happy songs on the ships deck.

As they got further from the waterfall, it got a little cooler. Johnny noticed that the red steamship was called The Recovery. When they were a safe distance from the waterfall, Porridge let a rope ladder down over the side. Johnny and Harry used this to climb on board The Recovery.

Up on deck, Johnny could see a lot further than from his little boat. In the distance, he could see a flagpole standing on a jetty. As they got closer, he could see that the jetty was made of wood and had been painted blue. The woods beyond the jetty looked very familiar. Johnny realised that he was back on the River Glee again.

The ship pulled in to the jetty. Johnny and the bears, still playing music, walked down the gangplank to the jetty. Porridge waved a silver conductors baton and the bears stopped playing. Then he spoke to Johnny.

"The next part of your journey is the most important one so far. You must remember all that you've learnt as you move on. It's time for you to get on…the Road to Recovery!" Porridge flourished his silver conductors baton (which had been a magic wand all along). The green grass by the edge of the River Glee began to smoulder with blue smoke.

A loud rumbling sound drowned out the birdsong in the trees and the ground shook. Johnny wasn't scared, because he saw that the bears weren't. They clutched each other for support, because the ground was shaking a lot, but giggled excitedly at the magic that Porridge was weaving.

The smoke cleared from the fields and Johnny saw a road that hadn't been there a minute ago. The road was made of shiny red and blue bricks, which reflected little rainbow patterns in the sunlight . The bricks looked smooth and well worn. By the side of the road was a signpost. It had one word painted on it next to an arrow pointing the direction : RECOVERY.

"This is your own personal Road to Recovery", said Porridge, in a voice that reminded him of the Teacher at School. "You must stay on the Road and not stray from it. No matter what temptations get in your way, just stay on the Road. When you've reached the end of it, you'll have reached Recovery and you won't be ill any more."

Johnny nodded his head eagerly. He was going to try his best to do what Porridge had told him to. Little Red shyly produced a tiny harp made of white enamel. She stroked its golden strings as she sang farewell to Johnny:

"You must be strong,

The road is very long

But don't despair,

Take it like a bear."

Her words faded away as Johnny set off on the Road to Recovery. Johnny looked over his shoulder to say goodbye to the bears, but they'd gone. He was on his own again. But Johnny shrugged his shoulders and carried on walking. He was on the Road to Recovery, he reminded himself with a smile.

On he walked, admiring the distant woodlands of Happy Valley until they vanished from sight. The grassy meadow also disappeared and were replaced by yellow sands. It reminded Johnny of the beach, but where was the sea? Nowhere in sight.

The sun changed colour, too. Instead of being its usual yellow, the sun had become red and was shimmering hotly in a blue haze. Johnny tried not to look at the sun, because it made him feel ill again. He began to feel very thirsty. His feet became very tired, as the bricks on the road were getting very warm and uncomfortable to walk on.

But Johnny kept walking. He knew that he was on the Road to Recovery and remembering that helped him to carry on.

Johnny had never been so thirsty in all his life. He was desperate for a drink of water. Or milk. Or squash. Or anything, so long as it was cold and wet.

In front of him, off the road, Johnny saw a fountain. Its jets of water rose upwards into the air before cascading into a deep blue pool of water at the fountains base. Johnny was tempted to run over and dive into the pool, head first, but he remembered Porridge's words. He must stay on the road. Or he wouldn't reach Recovery and would stay ill.

He stayed on the road and kept walking. As he walked, he got thirstier and thirstier. He turned back to look at the fountain, hoping that this would cool him down, but it had vanished.

On he walked with a hot throat and a dry mouth. Then Johnny looked down and saw something sticking out of the pocket of his pajama jacket. It was a magic wand, made of green wood. Johnny waved his wand in the air and silently wished for a drink.

A silver tray carrying a jug of lemonade and a glass appeared magically in front of him. Johnny poured himself a drink and drank it in one gulp. He had another glass. Then a third. No longer thirsty, Johnny walked on.

Soon he became very hungry. His tummy started to rumble loudly. On and on he walked, getting hungrier and hungrier. Then he remembered his magic wand. He waved it, but the food that he wished for didn't appear.

A short distance from the road ahead stood a large apple tree. Its branches were bending under the weight of hundreds of big red apples. They shone in the sunlight and looked very tasty. Johnny was about to run to the tree and help himself to apples, but he remembered Porridge's warning. He still couldn't leave the road or he wouldn't reach Recovery.

But he did have an idea. He waved his magic wand again and wished for an apple. A large apple flew slowly from the tree, across the desert, and hovered in front of Johnny as he stood on the road. He ate it hungrily. It was sweet and juicy, just like the apples in the garden at home. It also stopped Johnny feeling hungry.

Johnny was not as tired now and strode on along the road. Not long now until Recovery, he told himself.

Then the road divided into two parts. One turned to the right, the other to the left. Johnny stood at the fork in the road, wondering which way to turn. He didn't want to take the wrong road, because then he'd never get to Recovery.

Johnny wished for some help. He waved his magic wand and stood back two steps. The two roads were hit by a fork of yellow lightning which stung Johnny's eyes. He rubbed his eyes slowly, to recover from the blinding lightning.

When he opened his eyes again, Johnny saw a single road in front of him. The other road had vanished and he was back on track. Back on the Road to Recovery.

Eagerly he walked on. He felt sure that he was almost there. But then the road disappeared. It just stopped. Johnny stood at the end of the road and a single, salty tear fell from his eye and down his cheek.

Then Johnny felt someone tap him on the shoulder. He turned around and there was Porridge with Harry, Red and all the other bears.

"Well done, Johnny!", cried Porridge excitedly. "You've made it. The Road to Recovery is at an end. Welcome to Recovery!"

Johnny looked around him. The road had disappeared and he was back in Happy Valley with the bears. He was no longer ill. He felt fine.

"If ever you're ill again, just remember everything that you've learnt here.", said Porridge. "And now it's time for you to go back and share the good news with Mummy and Daddy."

Harry jumped up into Johnny's arms. Although he like being in Happy Valley with the other bears, he wanted to go home again with Johnny.

The other bears started sneezing. They sneezed very loudly. A wind blew from behind them, blowing orange and brown leaves into Johnny's and Harry's faces. There were so many leaves that Johnny couldn't see the other bears.

Then Johnny woke up in bed. His bedspread was over his head. As he removed the bedclothes from over his head, Johnny noticed that the bedclothes were jumbled up together. He must have had a difficult nights sleep, he thought to himself.

Later that morning, the Doctor called in and told Johnny that he was no longer ill and was better again. How Johnny whooped and cheered!

In the afternoon after lunch, Johnny was allowed into the garden for the first time in ages. He felt the wind in his hair again. He didn't feel strong enough to ride his bike, but enjoyed seeing the red frame shining in the sunlight. He could hear the birds singing more clearly than when he was in bed. The song of his favourite robin redbreast sounded best of all.

Johnny sat on a chair under the apple tree with Harry by his side. The wind blew gently in his face. All his troubles were now gone, he felt. Harry and his friends in Happy Valley had helped him leave all his cares behind.

He felt good to be alive.

The End